One morning a long time ago, clever Jackal was out looking for food. The food he liked best was roast chicken, but a plump lizard was good, too.

As Jackal ambled along, he sniffed and smelled the sweet smell of lizards on the breeze.

“Mmmmmm, I do like a good, fat lizard,” he said to himself, licking his lips.

The smell led him down into a deep valley with steep sides. It was quite dark in the valley. Only a little sunshine came down that far.

Suddenly, Jackal heard something ahead of him. Was it a lizard? It sounded big!

But it was not a lizard...

The King of the Savanna stood before him, snarling, and blocking the track. His big, white teeth glinted in the sunshine.

“Mmmmmm, I do like a good, fat jackal,” said the King, licking his lips.

Jackal was terrified. He looked all around, but there was no escape.

Then Jackal looked up. There was a big, flat rock hanging out across the valley. It was attached to the side of a cliff, but it looked like it was falling… Instantly a plan formed in clever Jackal's head.

Jackal flung himself down on the track.

"Help!" he cried, looking up at the rock, and then at the King. "That rock is about to fall on us! We shall be crushed!"

The King of the Savanna looked up at the rock. It loomed over him. It looked heavy.

"Quickly, good King!" said Jackal. "Use your incredible strength to hold up the rock!"

Without thinking, the King leapt under the rock and stretched out his arms to hold it up.

It was extremely heavy! The King's legs trembled.

"I cannot hold it much longer," he wailed. "What can we do?"

“Do not worry, good King,” said Jackal. “I will go and fetch a log to prop up the rock, and we will be saved.”

With that, Jackal scampered off along the track.

He ran up the side of the valley and onto the clifftop.

And then he kept on running.

"Just keep running," he panted to himself.

Soon he was far from the valley and the King and the big, flat rock.

He found himself a good fat lizard, and he ate it in the sunshine. It was sweet and yummy.

As he ate, Jackal chuckled to himself.

“The King is strong, but he is not clever. He will be under that rock for a long time before he learns that it is not falling!”